Richard Wagner, Alfred Forman

Parsifal in English verse

Richard Wagner, Alfred Forman

Parsifal in English verse

ISBN/EAN: 9783742849342

Manufactured in Europe, USA, Canada, Australia, Japa

Cover: Foto ©Andreas Hilbeck / pixelio.de

Manufactured and distributed by brebook publishing software
(www.brebook.com)

Richard Wagner, Alfred Forman

Parsifal in English verse

Parsifal

IN ENGLISH VERSE

FROM THE GERMAN OF
RICHARD WAGNER

BY

ALFRED FORMAN

TRANSLATOR OF "DER RING DES NIBELUNGEN,"
"TRISTAN UND ISOLDE," ETC.

LONDON · MDCCCXCIX: PRINTED FOR THE TRANSLATOR BY PRIVATE SUBSCRIPTION, AND ISSUED WITH THE CONSENT OF MESSRS. SCHOTT & CO., REGENT STREET.

TO FRIENDS IN BAYREUTH.

> " Nun danket Gott,
> dass ihr berufen ihn zu hören !"
>
> *Parsifal.*

You favoured few, from out a world of men,
Chosen to meet once more upon the ground
Where music then its utmost glory found
When Brünnhild' built her pyre and, in the ken
Of Gods and mortals, gave the Rhine again
His ravished gold !   I sit like one a-dream
And strain the soul of fancy till I seem
To reach your hearts, unhelped of speech or pen.
My blessing take, within the solemn halls
That rose to magic in its fulness near
Amphion's own what time the Theban walls
He built with stones that lent him living ear. —
But linger not ! The Grail-King's trumpet calls,
In strains, alas ! I am not bid to hear.

A. F.

London, Summer, 1886.

TRANSLATOR'S NOTE.

OVER the proof-sheets of the following translation some discussion with a valued friend arose as to the employment of certain words : *Saver* instead of *Saviour*, for instance ; *unmuffle* instead of *uncover*; *holy* instead of *sacred*. It may therefore (as he is probably not alone in his way of thinking) not be irrelevant if I here introduce the letter which I wrote to Wagner in 1873, accompanying a copy of my privately printed version of " Die Walküre." In this letter will be found some indication of the considerations which influenced the choice of vocabulary, as also some idea of the general principle worked upon in all my Wagner-translations. The letter ran as follows :

" I undertook the enclosed translation of ' Die Walküre' partly to gratify my own intense sympathy with your artistic aims in general, my deep interest in the intended performance of ' Der Ring des Nibelungen' at Bayreuth, and my love for your works as far as I have been able to make acquaintance with them in England, and partly for the benefit of a small circle of friends who are unable to read it in German. When I had completed it, it occurred to me that it might further be made useful for spreading in this country a knowledge of your works, and I therefore have had about two hundred copies printed, which, if in accordance with your wish, I should be glad to place at the disposal (for free distribution) of Mr. Dannreuther, or anyone else connected with the Wagner Society here whom you might please to point out to me. If you approve of this translation of the ' Walküre,' my *hope* is that I shall be able to gain time from my other occupations to complete the 'Ring' with similar translations of the 'Rheingold,' 'Siegfried,' and 'Götterdämmerung,' which might then be published in proper book-form. Moreover, I trust that the day is not distant when an edition of the music with English words will become necessary. My aim has been to produce a translation that shall appear as *poetry* to *English* readers. I have therefore considered it necessary to adhere to the poetical form and alliterative verse of the German. I have likewise endeavoured, as much as *possible* in our composite language, to avoid the use of such words as would too openly betray their Greek or Latin origin, as unfitted to the tone and subject of the drama. Beyond this, I have compared the whole with the music, and I think a very few alterations of the words would fit them to appear with the score. If, compelled by the necessities just mentioned, I have sometimes departed from your *words* farther than I should have wished, I trust that I have never gone far from your *thought*, and I feel that, under any circumstances, the translation as it now stands would give to English readers a more faithful idea of your drama than any prose word-for-word rendering that *I* could have made. If I have anywhere sinned against your meaning, correct me if you think my labour worthy of correction, and, if not, at least forgive the trespasses of a work of love."

However the case may be judged to stand with the vocabulary of the following version of " Parsifal," it was undertaken in the same spirit of profound devotion to the work itself, which led me to translate the " Ring des Nibelungen" and " Tristan und Isolde," and whatever acceptance the present volume may meet, I must always count my labours as amply repaid in the recognition accorded me by the Master himself. In the case of " Parsifal" I had the inestimable advantage, in the spring of 1877, of hearing it read by Wagner to a very small audience collected at the house of my friend Mr. Edward Dannreuther, in Orme Square. There, too, it had occurred to Wagner that the reading would be of greater interest to me if I were enabled to make a previous acquaintance with the play ; and it rests among my most precious memories that the MS. was placed in my possession for study before the reading took place. The drama was published in December, 1877; and my translation was finished in July, 1878. The reasons which have kept it so long unprinted I need not here explain.

The days of Wagner-introductions are (or should be) over, and I would further merely call attention to a point frequently missed by those who have not yet witnessed a stage-performance of " Parsifal." Kundry, it should be borne in mind, is a creature of two existences, one of subjection to Klingsor and one of voluntary service to the Grail, and sleeping and waking are the doors by which she passes from one state to the other.

The version here presented is not intended to be taken in strict and continuous (syllable-for-note) company with the music, and I have not considered it necessary to print the numerous alternative readings which would be requisite for such a purpose. The text used is that of the First Edition, 1877.

ALFRED FORMAN.

PERSONS OF THE DRAMA.

AMFORTAS.

TITUREL.

GURNEMANZ.

PARSIFAL.

KLINGSOR.

KUNDRY.

KNIGHTS AND SQUIRES OF THE GRAIL.

KLINGSOR'S WONDER-MAIDENS.

PLACE OF THE ACTION : in the realm and castle (" Monsalvat ") of the Grail-keepers ; landscape such as characterizes the northerly mountains of Gothic Spain. Then : Klingsor's Wonder-castle, assumed to be on the southern slope of the same mountains, facing towards Arabian Spain. The dress of the Knights and Squires of the Grail similar to that of the Order of Templars : white tabards and mantles ; instead, however, of the red cross, scutcheons and mantles embroidered with a hovering dove.

FIRST ACT.

Forest, shady and solemn, but not gloomy. Rocky ground. A clearer space in the midst. On the left the path to the Grailcastle is supposed to rise. In the direction of the middle of the background the stage slopes downwards towards a lower-lying forest-lake. — Daybreak. — Gurnemanz (grayheaded and hale) and two Squires (in early youth) are lying asleep under a tree. — From the left side, as if from the Grailcastle, is heard the solemn morning-call of the Trumpets.

GURNEMANZ

(arousing himself and shaking the squires).

Hey! Ho! Wood-keepers you!
Sleep-keepers in couple!
Yet waken at least o' the morning!

(The two squires leap up and sink, ashamed, immediately again on their knees.)

Hear you the cry? Now thanks to God,
that you are called of him to hear it!

(He sinks on his knees beside them; they perform their morning prayer together in silence; as soon as the trumpets cease, they rise.)

1

Now up, you youngsters; see to the bath;
the King, 't is time to wait for yonder:
before the litter, in which he rides,
I see the whifflers already near.
(*Two Knights enter from the direction of the castle.*)
Hail ye!   How fares Amfortas to-day?
He seeks the bath betimes this morning;
    the herb-cure, that Gawain
with craft and boldness went to gain,
I deem it brought his illness ease?

THE FIRST KNIGHT.

So deem'st thou, who yet knowest all?
    It but more burningly soon
    brought back the pangs again:
    worn with the sleepless sore
he urged us loudly for the bath.

GURNEMANZ
(*mournfully shaking his head*).

But fools we are if ease at all we hope for,
    where nought but healing eases!
For every herb, for every water, seek
    and hunt wide through the world:
      one thing, one wight —
      alone can help him.

FIRST KNIGHT.

Who is he, say!

GURNEMANZ
(*evasively*).
Look to the bath!

THE FIRST SQUIRE

(after turning with the second squire towards the background, looking to the right).

See yonder the headlong horsewoman !

SECOND SQUIRE.

Hei !
How the mane of her hell-filly leaps in the wind !

FIRST SQUIRE.

Yes ! Kundry 't is.

SECOND SQUIRE.

She carries weighty tidings ?

FIRST SQUIRE.

Giddy the mare is.

SECOND SQUIRE.

Flew she through the air ?

FIRST SQUIRE.

Now skims she the ground.

SECOND SQUIRE.

With her mane she brushes the moss.

FIRST SQUIRE.

Now wildly the woman alights.

(Kundry rushes, almost staggering, in. Wild clothing, looped up short ; girdle of snake-skins hanging far down ; black hair flowing in loose strings ; deep ruddy-brown complexion ; glittering black eyes, at times flashing wildly but for the most part vacant and fixed. — She goes swiftly to Gurnemanz and thrusts upon him a small crystal vessel.)

KUNDRY.

Here take it!—Balsam!

GURNEMANZ.

From whence this hast thou brought?

KUNDRY.

From further hence than thy thought can count:
    helps not this balsam here,
        Arabia holds
nought left that can do him good. —
Ask no further! — I am weary.

(She flings herself on the ground.)

(A train of squires and knights, carrying and accompanying the litter in which Amfortas lies stretched, arrives, from the left, upon the stage. — Gurnemanz has immediately turned from Kundry towards the new-comers.)

GURNEMANZ

(during their arrival).

He comes: behold they bring him hither. —
Ah, woe! How sore I feel the doom,
him, in his manhood's risen bloom,
the over-ruling race's lord,
slave of his sickness thus to see!

(To the squires.)

Be heedful! Hark, how groans the King.

(They halt and set down the litter.)

AMFORTAS

(who has slightly raised himself).

Enough ! — Have thanks ! — A little rest ! —
After a night of frantic pain,
now morning-forest-gleam again ;
  the holy lake
will likewise to my blood bring back the powers ;
  faint grows my ache,
  its night less darkly lowers. —
Gawain !

FIRST KNIGHT.

  Lord, Gawain waited not.
  Soon as the herb he brought,
  though sore in its quest he had smarted,
  was seen to fail thy hope,
on search again in haste away he started.

AMFORTAS.

Without my leave ? — Now ill betide him,
who Grail's-behest so light could rate !
Woe to his rashness, if it guide him
to where the snares of Klingsor wait !
So let by none the peace be broken :
I wait for him of whom the word was spoken —
  " by fellow-pain who knows " —
Was't not so ?

GURNEMANZ.

To us thou told'st it so.

AMFORTAS.

"the spotless fool" — —:
I know him, methinks, ere I meet him : —
O might I as Death but greet him!

GURNEMANZ.

But first, behold : with this yet make a trial !

(*He hands him the phial.*)

AMFORTAS

(*looking at it*).

Whence came this outland-looking flask ?

GURNEMANZ.

For thee it from Arabia has been fetched.

AMFORTAS.

And who has brought it ?

GURNEMANZ.

Here lies she, the wandering woman. —
Up, Kundry ! come !

(*She refuses.*)

AMFORTAS.

Thou, Kundry ?
Have I once more to thank thee,
thou wild unresting work-maid ?
So be !
This balsam here I yet will try,
if but in thanks for thy faithful toil !

KUNDRY

(lying restlessly on the ground).

No thanks! — Ha ha! How will it help thee?
No thanks! Forth, forth! To the bath!

(Amfortas gives the signal to proceed: he and his attendants disappear towards the lower background. — Gurnemanz, looking mournfully after them, and Kundry, still lying on the ground, remain behind. — Squires walk up and down.)

THIRD SQUIRE

(a young man).

Hi! Thou there! —
Why lie'st thou here like a desert beast?

KUNDRY.

Are the beasts then here not holy?

THIRD SQUIRE.

Yes; but if holy thou,
not yet have we rightly heard.

FOURTH SQUIRE

(also a young man).

She, with her wonder-juices, I fancy,
is like to make an end of the Master.

GURNEMANZ.

H'm! — Has she ever worked you harm? —
When all bewildered stand,
in farthest of lands to our fighting brothers
how to forward our tidings,
and scarce where they are can tell —

who is it, ere yet you have even bethought you,
storms off and thither comes and is back,
and has left the word that our brothers lack ?
You feed her not, nor house her head,
 in nothing with you she shares ;
but when in a danger help you need,
with zeal, on the wind, she almost flies,
and never for thanks or guerdon cries.
 Methinks if harm is in it,
 't were good for you to win it !

Third Squire.

 Yet hates she us. —
See how she spitefully watches us now !

Fourth Squire.

A heathen she is, a working witch.

Gurnemanz.

Yes, bound in a curse she well may be,
 here now on earth
 by later birth,
till blame away from her be driven
of former life yet unforgiven.
Seeks she of sin to loose the fetter
by deeds for which we fare the better,
't is clearly good she follows thus,
who helps herself and works for us.

Third Squire.

And may't not be that guilt of hers
which oft has brought us so much ill ?

GURNEMANZ.

Yes, often when afar from us she stayed,
 an evil over us has come.
   And long I now have known her;
   still longer knows her Titurel:
when here our fortress he was raising,
asleep he found her in the woods,
   breathless and stiffened as dead.
And so myself I found her lately,
when hardly had the evil happed,
which yonder wizard over the mountain
so blackly brought upon us all. —

    (*To Kundry.*)

Hi! Thou! — Hear me, and say;
where strayed thy feet about the world,
the day our Master lost the spear? —

    (*Kundry is silent.*)

Why had we from thee then no help?

KUNDRY.

I never help.

FOURTH SQUIRE.

She says it herself.

THIRD SQUIRE.

Is she so true and bold in fence,
for the spear we lost why send her not hence?

GURNEMANZ

(*gloomily*).

Another matter ! —
To all it is forbid. —

(*With great emotion.*)

Wound-wonder-filled
and holy-holden spear !
I saw thee grasped
in all-ungodly hand ! —

(*Yielding to his recollections.*)

When armed with it, Amfortas, first in daring,
who back could hold thee so
before the wizard-foe ? —
The hero, near the gate, was drawn apart ;
a woman, dreadly fair, bewitched his heart ;
upon her bosom lies he drunken,
the spear from his hand is sunken ; —
a deadly cry ! — to him I fly ; —
with laughter Klingsor went from sight,
the holy spear was in his might.
With sword and shield I helped the King's escaping ;
but in his side a fiery wound was gaping : —
the wound it is that closes not again.

THIRD SQUIRE.

So knew'st thou Klingsor ?

GURNEMANZ

(*to the first and second squires who come from the lake*).

With the King how fares it ?

Second Squire.

The bath has eased him.

First Squire.

The balsam stayed the pain.

Gurnemanz

(*after a silence*).

The wound it is that closes not again! —

Third Squire.

But, father, speak and tell it me ;
thou knewest Klingsor, — how can it be ?

(*The third and fourth squires had already seated themselves at Gurnemanz's feet; the two others now take up their place beside them.*)

Gurnemanz.

Titurel, the godly hero,
    he knew him well.
To him, when foes had made with craft and might
    the realm of true believers waver,
to him came down, in holy noiseless night,
    the blessèd servers of the Saver:
the cup whose draught at his last meal he swallowed,
the hallowed bowl in which, as after followed,
upon the cross he shed his heavenly blood,
the spear as well whose point had drawn its flood, —
the highest wealth of all the witness-things, —
they gave to be a treasure of our King's.
To hold the relics he upreared the shrine.

You all, who flocked to our Beginner
by paths where never walks a sinner,
        you know that only he
        of spotless heart is free
to join the breth'ren whom the Grail asunder
has called for saving work and strengthened with its wonder;
to him it was, of whom you ask, forbid —
Klingsor — though mighty toil for it he did.
As hermit yonder dwelt he in the valley,
behind it, wide and rich, lies heathenland:
I knew not what the sin that weighed upon him;
but shrift now sought he, and would fain be holy.
Unable in his soul the rooted sin to smother,
bane on himself with felon hand he wrought,
        which, after, tow'rds the Grail outstraught,
with scorn its holy keeper thrust aside;
whereon his wrath to Klingsor grew a guide —
        from his deed of shameful sacrifice
        how wisdom of wicked spells might rise;
            which now he found: —
the waste he made a gardenland of blisses,
        where fair and fiendish women flower,
in hope to snare the Grailhood with their kisses
        and thrall it deep in devils'-power;
who yields, to hold him fast knows Klingsor how,
and many he has wrecked for us ere now. —
When Titurel, with hoary age fordone,
had yielded here the lordship to his son,
        Amfortas, on an early day,
        this wizard-plague set out to stay;
        what then befell you have been told;
        the spear is now in Klingsor's hold;

and with it since our saints themselves he pierces,
to gain the Grail a steadfast hope he nurses.

(*Kundry during this speech has shown frequent signs of violent agitation.*)

FOURTH SQUIRE.

Then first of all the spear must back be won!

THIRD SQUIRE.

Both weal and fame were his by whom 't were done!

GURNEMANZ

(*after a silence*).

At the bereaved and darkened shrine
in burning prayer was stretched Amfortas,
of healing to behold some token;
light from the Grail streamed softly out unfettered:
a holy dream-sight then
said clearly to his ken
in word-show plainly out before him lettered: —
"the spotless fool
by fellow-pain who knows;
wait for him,
whom I forechose."

(*With great solemnity the four squires repeat the saying.*)

(*From the direction of the lake are heard shouts and cries of*)

THE KNIGHTS AND SQUIRES.

Woe! Woe! — Ho ho!
Help! — Who can have done it?

(*Gurnemanz and the four squires start and turn round in alarm. — A wild swan with failing flight flutters in from the lake; it is wounded, can scarcely support itself and at last sinks dying to the ground. — Meanwhile :*)

GURNEMANZ.

What is 't ?

FIRST SQUIRE.
Yonder!

SECOND SQUIRE.
Here!   A swan.

THIRD SQUIRE.

A wild swan!

FOURTH SQUIRE.
And behold it wounded !

OTHER SQUIRES
(*rushing in from the lake*).

Ha!   Woe!   Woe!

GURNEMANZ.
Who shot the swan ?

THE SECOND KNIGHT
(*coming forward*).
The King as a happy token hailed it,
while round above the lake it flew ;
then came a dart . . .

FRESH SQUIRES
(*dragging Parsifal forward*).

He 't was!   He shot!   Here the arrow,
made like his!   And here the bow !

GURNEMANZ

(*to Parsifal*).

Is't thou by whom this swan was slaughtered?

PARSIFAL.

Why yes! I shoot whatever may fly.

GURNEMANZ.

Thou did'st the deed? And feelest no dread in thy heart?

THE SQUIRES.

Woe to the slayer!

GURNEMANZ.

Wild unheard-of work!
To come with murder here in the holy forest,
whose blessèd peace was round thee spread!
The woodland beasts, they came not to thee tame?
Looked they not harmless and kind?
From the branches what warbled to thee the birds?
How hurt thee the trusty swan?
In search of his mate aloft he rose,
to wheel beside her over the lake,
which so he turns to a holy healing bath.
It gave thee no thrill? It led thee but
to rash and boylike work with thy bow? —
Our friend he was: what is he now to thee?
Here — behold — here struck'st thou him:
here thickens the blood, hang faintly the feathers;
the snowy wings with darkness are flecked, —
his eye-light fades; see'st thou the look? —
Grows there a sense of thy sin within thee?

(Parsifal has listened to him with growing signs of emotion; he now breaks his bow and flings his arrows from him.)

Speak, boy! and own thy all-unbounded fault!

(Parsifal draws his hand over his eyes.)

What gave thee the heart to do it?

PARSIFAL.

I knew of it not.

GURNEMANZ.

Whence com'st thou here?

PARSIFAL.

I cannot tell.

GURNEMANZ.

Who is thy father?

PARSIFAL.

I cannot tell.

GURNEMANZ.

Who bade thee to come this way?

PARSIFAL.

I know not.

GURNEMANZ.

Then what thy name?

PARSIFAL.

I once had many,
but none of them any longer I know.

GURNEMANZ.

All this thou knowest nought of?

(*To himself.*)

So dull as he
I none but Kundry ever found. —

(*To the squires, whose number has been gradually increasing.*)

Now go!
And let the King at his bath not wait!—

(*Pointing to the swan.*)

Help!

(*The squires reverently take up the swan, and disappear with it towards the lake.*)

GURNEMANZ

(*turning again to Parsifal*).

Now speak! Nought know'st thou that I ask thee:
then tell me what thou know'st;
of something thou must have knowledge.

PARSIFAL.

I have a mother; Herzeleid' is her name:
in woods and on hedgeless meadows had we our home.

GURNEMANZ.

Who gave thee thy bow?

PARSIFAL.

I made it myself,
to fright the savage birds in the forest.

GURNEMANZ.

Yet lordly thou seem'st to be and high of birth:

why was it now that thy mother
taught thee no seemlier weapons ?
(*Parsifal is silent.*)

Kundry

(*who, lying at the edge of the wood, has kept her look keenly
fixed on Parsifal, breaks roughly in*).

No father he had when his mother bore him,
for in fight fresh-slain was Gamuret ;
from such an early hero-death
her son to shelter, far from weapons
a fool in the wilds she brought him up —
the fool herself !
(*She laughs.*)

Parsifal

(*who, with sudden interest, has been listening*).

Yes !   And once along the edge of the wood
on shapely beasts there came
a line of glittering riders ;
I wanted to be like them ;
they laughed and hasted away.
I ran behind but could not overtake them ;
through wilderness went I, up hill, down vale ;
it oft was night, then day again ;
my bow I needed to help me
against beasts and manlike monsters.

Kundry

(*warmly*).

Yes, robbers and giants can tell of his might :
the boy with his bow they found to be fearful

PARSIFAL.

Who fears me then ?   Say !

KUNDRY.

The wicked.

PARSIFAL.

The men who threatened me, wicked were they ?
(*Gurnemanz laughs.*)
Who is <u>good</u> ?

GURNEMANZ

(*gravely*).

Thy mother whom thou hast fled from,
and who for loss of thee weeps and grieves.

KUNDRY.

Her grief is done, for his mother is dead.

PARSIFAL

(*in fearful dread*).

Dead ? — My mother ? — Who said it ?

KUNDRY.

I rode therepast, and die I beheld her:
to thee, the fool, I bring her greeting.

(*Parsifal, in rage, leaps on Kundry and seizes her by the throat.*)

GURNEMANZ

(*holding him off*).

Mad-headed youngster !   Murder again ?
How hurt thee the woman ?   She told the truth.
For never lies Kundry, though much she has seen.

(After Gurnemanz has freed Kundry from his grasp, Parsifal stands for some time as if dazed; he is then seized with violent trembling.)

PARSIFAL.

I am faint and giddy! —

(Kundry goes swiftly to a stream, brings water in a horn, with which she first sprinkles Parsifal, and then hands it to him to drink.)

GURNEMANZ.

'T is well!   The Grail's behest she follows :
he heals an ill who pays it with good.

KUNDRY

(turning sadly away).

Good do I never ; — I want but rest.

(While Gurnemanz is tending Parsifal with fatherly care, Kundry, unobserved by both, slips into a thicket.)

But rest!   But rest . . . for brain and body! —
Sleep! sleep! — And oh, that none may wake me!
(Starting in terror.)
No!   Not sleep! — With dread I shudder!

(After a muffled cry she is seized with violent trembling; she then lets her arms sink faintly down, droops her head, and staggers away a little further.)

Fruitless the fence!   The time is here.
And sleep — and sleep — I must.

(She sinks down among the bushes and from this moment remains unnoticed.   A stir is heard from the direction of the lake, and in the background is seen the train of knights and squires returning homewards with the litter.)

GURNEMANZ.

The King has left the lake for home:
    high stands the sun;
now let me to our love-meal lead thee;
    for, — art thou pure,
the Grail will slake thy thirst and feed thee.

(He has laid Parsifal's arm softly round his own neck and places his own arm round Parsifal's body; in this manner he leads him by slow degrees along.)

PARSIFAL.

Who is the Grail?

GURNEMANZ.

    That tell we not;
but if thou hast to Him been bidden,
from thee the news will stay not hidden. —
    And see!
Thy face methinks I rightly knew:
the land no path to Him leads through;
and search but severs from Him wider,
when He himself is not its guider.

PARSIFAL.

I hardly walk, —
yet seem to move apace.

GURNEMANZ.

Thou see'st, my son,
here time is turned to space.

(Gradually and imperceptibly, while Gurnemanz and Parsifal appear to walk, the scene is changed from left to right: the forest disappears: a passage is opened in a wall of rock into which they seem to pass; they then again become visible in ascending galleries, through which they apparently move. —

*Long-drawn trumpet-cries swell softly on the ear : approaching
sound of bells. — At last they arrive in a vast hall which rises
into a high-vaulted dome through which alone comes the light. —
From the height above the dome the bells grow louder and
louder.)*

GURNEMANZ

(turning to Parsifal who stands as if spell-struck).

Now watch with heed ; and let me learn,
  if spotless and a fool thou be,
what knowledge is at least allowed to thee. —

*(At each side of the background a large door is opened. From
the right the Knights of the Grail, in solemn procession, enter
and, in course of the singing which follows, range themselves by
degrees at two large covered tables which are so placed that,
running parallel to each other from back to front, they leave the
middle of the hall free : cups only are upon them.)*

THE KNIGHTS OF THE GRAIL.

Who day by day is able
to look on as his last
the love-meal on the table
at which he stays his fast,
who joys in deeds of good,
for him be bread renewed :
his want he here may slake,
the godly gift may take.

YOUNGER MEN'S VOICES

(heard from the mid-height of the hall).

For worlds of sin,
  in torturing flood
as once his life was poured,

from deep within
now yearns my blood
to flow for Christ our Lord.
The flesh he deigned for us to give,
by death of him in us shall live.

Boys' Voices

(from the extreme height of the dome).

Faith beams above,
down wings the dove
by the Saver sent to speed you,
who knows when wine
in your cup should shine
and bread of life should feed you.

(Through the opposite door Amfortas is brought in on a litter by squires and serving brothers : before him walk boys carrying a casket covered with crimson hangings. This procession goes to the middle of the background where, under a canopy, stands a raised couch upon which Amfortas is set down from the litter: in front of it stands an altar-like oblong marble table upon which the boys place the veiled casket. — When the singing is ended and all the knights have taken their places at the tables there is lengthened silence. — From a vaulted niche in the furthest background, behind the couch of Amfortas, is heard, as if out of a tomb, the voice of the aged)

Titurel.

My son Amfortas ! Hast thou begun ?
(Silence.)
Shall I the Grail to-day behold and live ?
(Silence.)
Am I to die unguided by the Saver ?

AMFORTAS

(in an outbreak of despairing anguish).

Woe to me, woe!   The throb!   The sting! —
    My father, oh! once further
    do thou the holy work!
Live! oh, live and let me die!

TITUREL.

The grave I live in by the Saver's name;
    but old and weak am I to serve him;
    by service wipe away thy blame! —
        Unmuffle the Grail!

AMFORTAS

(restraining the boys).

No!   Leave it from me shut! — Oh! —
By none, by none can measured be the pang
I suffer at the sight that feeds your souls! —
What is the wound and what its burning bite
    beside this hell that harrows me,
    to such a work so . . . cursed to be! —
Woefullest guerdon to me its winner!
I, only of all, the single sinner,
    to serve the shrine before my brothers
and pray its blessing down on sinless others! —
Oh, stroke more dread than ever yet did spring
from heav'n's at length offended Mercy-King! —
    For Him and for his holy greeting
        I yearn with thirst like fire;
    by penance only comes the meeting . . .
        and deepest heart's-desire : —
        the hour is near :—
the gleam floats down upon the holy work;

the veil is dropped :
the blood of heav'n within the vessel's deep
in flame is lifted from its sleep ;
pierced with the smart of joy's all-blessèd taste,
the flush of the holy flood —
into my heart I feel it haste :
the wave of my body's own sinful blood
to flight headlong is hurled,
in whirl-streams back it is given
to the sin-ward-yearning world,
in wild unwillingness driven ; —
afresh it forces the door
whence now it begins to pour,
here from the wound, the like of His,
which doing of the selfsame weapon is
that gave the Redeemer his gaping bane,
from which in bloody rivers
He wept with the fulness of fellow-pain
for men his murder-givers ; —
and from which in me, at holiest hour,
the God-sent chattels' guarder,
the salvation-balsam's warder,
the burning sinner-blood is launched,
fresh from the seething well whose shower
is, ah ! by no penance to be staunched !
Have mercy ! Have mercy !
Fount of mercy, show me mercy !
From my birthright unbind me,
healed let me die,
that pure thou may find me
when brought to thine eye !
(*He sinks back as if unconscious.*)

Boys' Voices
(*out of the dome*).

" The spotless fool
by fellow-pain who knows ;
    wait for him,
    whom I forechose."

The Knights
(*softly*).

So sent thee was the message,
    wait without fear ;
the service do to-day !

Titurel's Voice.
Unmuffle the Grail !

(*Amfortas has silently raised himself again. The boys uncover the golden casket, take out of it the " Grail" (an antique crystal cup), from which they also remove a veil, and set it in front of Amfortas.*)

Titurel's Voice.
The blessing !

(*While Amfortas in solemn speechless prayer bends down to the cup, a gradually increasing gloom is spread through the hall.*)

Boys
(*from the dome*).

" Take and drink my blood,
    for sake of love between us !
Take and eat my flesh,
    and so forget me never ! "

(*A dazzling beam of light falls from above upon the cup, which glows with a stronger and stronger crimson hue.*)

Amfortas, with transfigured mien, lifts the " Grail" on high and waves it softly in all directions. The whole company, as the gloom came on, had fallen on their knees, and now raise their looks, with devotion, to the " Grail.")

TITUREL'S VOICE.

Oh ! Holiest bliss !
How clearly greets us the Master to-day !

(Amfortas puts down the " Grail," which now, as the gloom passes away, grows paler and paler : hereupon the boys shut the vessel again in the casket which they cover as before. — With the return of the previous daylight the cups, now filled with wine, again become visible upon the tables; beside each lies a small loaf of bread. All sit down to the meal, including Gurnemanz, who keeps a place at his side empty and signals to Parsifal to sit and partake of the meal : Parsifal, however, as if completely in a trance, remains aside moveless and dumb.)

(Alternate singing during the meal.)

BOYS' VOICES

(from the height).

Wine and bread of his last board
once the Grail's belovèd Lord,
by might of love and fellow-pain,
turned to blood he yielded up,
to flesh he offered, for our gain.

YOUNG MEN'S VOICES

(from the mid-height).

Blood and flesh, which then he spent,
are turned, that strength to you be sent,

by comfort-spell and saviour-sway,
into wine, that fills your cup,
into bread you eat to-day.

THE KNIGHTS
(*first half*).

Eat of the bread,
turn it with speed
to body's strength and fitness ;
of death without dread,
of toils without heed,
that by works for the Lord you may witness.

(*Second half.*)

Drink of the wine,
change it anew
to blood that will fill you like fire ;
with gladness for sign,
to brotherhood true,
that in fight you may turn not or tire.

(*They rise solemnly from their seats and give each other their hands.*)

ALL THE KNIGHTS.

Blessèd in faith !
Blessèd in love !

YOUTHS
(*from the mid-height*).

Blessèd in love !

BOYS
(*from the height*).

Blessèd in faith !

(*During the meal, of which he did not partake, Amfortas has gradually relapsed from his state of exaltation: he bends his head and holds his hand upon the wound. The boys approach him; their movements indicate the renewed bleeding of the wound: they tend Amfortas, help him again to the litter, and, while all make ready for departure, they carry, in the order in which they came, Amfortas and the holy casket from the hall. The knights and squires also form themselves again in solemn procession and slowly leave the hall, from which the hitherto existing daylight gradually wanes. The bells have again sounded. — Parsifal, at the loudest foregoing outcry of Amfortas, had made a vehement movement with his hand towards his heart which he for some time pressed convulsively: he now remains standing stupefied and motionless in his place. — When the last have left the hall and again shut the doors, Gurnemanz walks ill-humouredly up to Parsifal and shakes him by the arm.*)

GURNEMANZ.

Why still standest thou here?
Know'st thou what thou saw'st?

(*Parsifal slightly shakes his head.*)

GURNEMANZ.

A fool thou art and nothing more!

(*He opens a narrow side-door.*)

Up now and out and hence away!
But put my word to use:
vex not the swans here again from to-day,
and seek, like a gander, thy goose!

(*He thrusts Parsifal out and slams the door angrily after him. As he, then, follows the knights, the curtain closes.*)

SECOND ACT.

....

Klingsor's Wonder-castle. — In the inner hold of a tower open towards the top; stone steps lead up to the battlements of the tower-wall; darkness in the depth towards which is a descent from the wall's projecture which is represented by the floor of the stage. Implements of witchcraft and necromantic utensils. -- Klingsor aside on the wall-projecture, sitting before a metal mirror.

KLINGSOR.

The time is here ! —
The fool my wonder-burg has lit on,
with boy's delight who shouting now is near. —
In sleep like death the curse yet holds her fast,
from whom its cramp to loose is mine. —
Up then !   To work !

(He steps towards the middle, a little lower down, and kindles incense which at once fills a part of the background with a bluish smoke. He then seats himself again in his former place and calls, with mysterious gestures, down into the depth :)

Aloft ! Hither ! To me !
Thou Nameless, heed thy master's power ;
she-fiend-of-old and devil's-flower !
Herodias wast thou, and what more ?
Gundryggia there, Kundry here.
Hither ! Hither then, Kundry !
To meet thy master, aloft !

(In midst of the bluish light appears the form of Kundry. She utters a horrible shriek like the cry of one half awaked in terror out of deep sleep.)

KLINGSOR.

Awak'st thou ? Ha !
To my spell thou fallest
once more to-day at fitting time.

(*Kundry raises a woeful howl which sinks by degrees from
extreme vehemence into a frightened whimpering.*)

Say, how far hast thou strayed to again ?
Fye ! Yonder, with the hero-herd,
where thou lettest thyself like a beast be kept ?
At my side here is it not better ?
The day thou caughtest for me their master —
ha ha ! — the spotless guard of the Grail, —
what hunted thee from me again so fast ?

KUNDRY

(*hoarsely and brokenly as if trying to regain the power of
speech*).

Ah ! — Ah !
Crushing night —
madness ! — Oh ! — Rage ! —
Oh ! Sorrow ! —
Sleep ! — Sleep —
Stifling sleep ! — Death !

KLINGSOR.

Yonder awoke thee another ? Eh ?

KUNDRY

(*as before*).

Yes ! — My curse ! —
Oh ! — The yearning — the yearning ! —

KLINGSOR.

Ha ha! — hence to the lustless heroes?

KUNDRY.

There — there — served I.

KLINGSOR.

Yes, yes! — to help undo the evil
     that thy spite had brought on their heads?
          They aid thee no whit:
          all can be bought,
     bid I the fitting price;
          the best of them fails,
     sinks he once on thy bosom:
     and is forfeit, so, to the spear
that from their master myself I snatched. —
With the dreadest of all to-day we must strive:
     him shelters foolhood's shield.

KUNDRY.

I — will not! — Oh! — Oh!

KLINGSOR.

Yet wilt thou, for thou must.

KUNDRY.

Thou — canst — not — hold me.

KLINGSOR.

But I can seize thee.

KUNDRY.

Thou?

Act II.

KLINGSOR.
>> Thy master.

KUNDRY.
> By might of what?

KLINGSOR.
> Ha! For only on me
> is thy might of no weight.

KUNDRY
(with shrill laughter).
> Ha! ha! — Art thou chaste?

KLINGSOR
(in rage).
Why asks me that thy cursèd mouth?
(He sinks into dismal thought.)
>> Harrowing need! —
> So mocks me the fiend to-day,
>> that for saint-hood I once should have striven!
>> Harrowing need!
Fleshly fever's all-torturing sway!
The hell, that to rise in my body was given,
that at last to the dumbness of death I had driven,
> here opens its grin at me wide
> through thee, thou devil's-bride! —
>> Heed thyself!
Scorn has by one been paid for already;
who, proud and strong in holiness,
> once thrust my hand aside;
> my pawn his tribe is,—

by his cureless wound
is the saint-chattels' Holder up-eaten ;
and soon — so seems it —
guard I myself the Grail. — —
Ha! Ha!
Was sweet to thee once Amfortas, the knight.
whom I lent thee to mix with in fellow-delight ?

KUNDRY.

Oh! — Torture! — Torture!
Faint even he! Faint they all are!
To my curse . . . with me . . .
all of them fallen! —
Oh! sleep without end,
my only weal,
how, -- how shall I win thee ?

KLINGSOR.

He, who withstands thee, frees thee as well :
so try with the youngster who nears !

KUNDRY.

I — will not!

KLINGSOR.

He climbs already the wall.

KUNDRY.

Oh, sorrow! Sorrow!
Awakened I for this ?
Must I ? — Must ?

KLINGSOR

(*who has mounted the tower-wall*).

Ha! — He is fair, the youngster !

KUNDRY.

Oh! — Oh! — Woe to me! —

KLINGSOR

(sounding a horn towards the outside).

Ho! Ho! — You watchmen! Hither!
Heroes! — Up! — Foes are near!

(Outside, a growing tumult and clash of weapons.)

Hei! — How they storm to the bulwark,
 the befooled and witch-worked poppets,
for fence of their fair sweethearting devils! —
 So! — Stoutly! — Stoutly!
 Ha ha! — He shows not a fear: —
the hero Ferris he sleights of his weapon,
and wields it like flame in face of the swarm. —

(Kundry begins to laugh uneasily.)

How ill to the blockheads has thriven their zeal!
One bleeds at the arm, another the leg.
 Ha ha! — They falter, they scatter;
each carries his hurt with him home! —
  How little I grudge it them!
  Would that this way
 swiftly by means of itself
 the whole of the knighthood were slaughtered. —
Ha! How proudly he stands on the wall-top!
How gleam his cheeks with the roses of laughter,
 while, wonder-struck like a child,
 the forsaken garden he scans! —
Hei! Kundry!

(He turns round. Kundry's laughter had grown more and more hysterical and ecstatic, and had at last passed into a convulsive and lamentable cry; her form has now entirely disappeared; the bluish light is extinguished: complete darkness in the depth.)

How? So soon at work? —
Ha ha! The spell I know of old,
that always to serve me fetches thee back. —
Thou there, — boy in thy bloom!
Whatever once
foretold to thee was, —
too young and raw
fall'st thou within my might :—
thy spotlessness once from thee driven,
to me thou for ever art given !

(He sinks slowly with the whole tower: at the same time rises the Wonder-garden and entirely fills the stage. Tropical vegetation, with richest splendour of flowers: towards the background a boundary is formed by the battlement of the castle-wall, on which abut, sideways, projectures from the castle itself (in rich Arabian style) with terraces. On the wall stands Parsifal looking with wonder down into the garden. — On all sides, both from the garden and the palace, rush in, in confusion, first singly, then in increasing numbers, a host of beautiful girls, their clothing hurriedly and lightly thrown on, as if they had just been startled from sleep.)

GIRLS

(coming from the garden).

Here was the uproar,
weapons, frantic noises !

GIRLS

(coming from the castle).

Woe and vengeance!   Up!
Where is the spoiler?

SOME OF THE GIRLS.

My beloved he has wounded.

OTHERS.

Mine too is missing!

OTHERS.

I awakened alone, —
where has he fled to?

OTHERS STILL.

There in the building? —
They bleed!   O sorrow!
Who is the foe? —
There stands he!   See! —
With my Ferris's sword? —
I saw it, the castle he stormed. —
I heard the master's horn.
My hero hither ran,
the others followed, but each
he met with a welcome of wounds.
    The daunter!   The frightener!
    All of them fled from him. —
    Thou there!   Thou there!
Why work for us all such a harm?
Our curse, our curse on thy head!

(Parsifal leaps a little lower into the garden.)

THE GIRLS.

Ha! Undoer! Dar'st thou to face us?
Why hurt'st thou so our belovèds?

PARSIFAL
(*in extreme surprise*).

You winsome children, to hurt them was I not bounden?
To your sweetness they struggled to bar my way.

GIRLS.

For us did'st thou seek?
Hast thou seen us before?

PARSIFAL.

I never beheld yet so dainty a throng;
fair if I call you, deem you me wrong?

THE GIRLS
(*passing from surprise into merriment*).

So art thou not come to harm us?

PARSIFAL.

Believe me, no.

GIRLS.

But the evil
thou did'st us is not to be meted, —
our playmates so to have treated:
who plays with us now?

PARSIFAL.

With gladness I.

THE GIRLS
(*laughing*).

If us thou art fain for, pass not by:
and of blame if thou spare us the burden,

we have for thee thy guerdon ;
for gold we do not play,
we look but to love for pay;
with it if thou soothe our trouble,
we back will yield it thee double.

(Some of them have gone into the thicket and now, as if clothed in flowers and themselves looking like flowers, come back again.)

THE FLOWER-DECKED GIRLS

(singly).

Back from the boy, thou ! — To me he belongs. —
No ! — No ! — To me ! — To me !

THE OTHER GIRLS.

Ah, the tricksters ! — To deck without telling !

(They disappear likewise and come quickly back again, dressed in the same manner, with flowers.)

THE GIRLS

(while, with childlike grace and merriment, they dance, in turns, round Parsifal, and softly caress his cheeks and chin).

Be mine ! Be mine !
Thou sweet new-comer,
in bloom before thee,
with breath like fresh'ning summer,
I waft my love-balm o'er thee.

PARSIFAL

(standing calmly and contentedly in their midst).

How sweetly you smell !
Are you then flowers ?

THE GIRLS

(sometimes singly, sometimes several together).

The garden we deck
and scent to it bring,
by the master plucked in the spring;
we ripen at beck
of summer and sun,
in bliss for thee blooming, each one.
Be good to us here to-day,
begrudge not the flowers their pay:
for bring'st thou not love to us hither,
away we shall dwindle and wither.

FIRST GIRL.

O take me to thy bosom!

SECOND.

With my touch let me cool thy brow!

THIRD.

Thy cheek let me smooth for thee now!

FOURTH.

Thy mouth let me close with my kisses!

FIFTH.

No, me! The fairest am I.

SIXTH.

No, I! My scent is the sweetest.

PARSIFAL

(softly repulsing their importunity).

You wild sweet crush of flower and flesh,
am I to play with you, loosen your mesh!

GIRLS.

Why scold us ?

PARSIFAL.

You keep not peace.

GIRLS.

Our strife is for thee.

PARSIFAL.

Then cease !

FIRST GIRL
(*to the second*).

Away from him !   Me he has chosen.

SECOND GIRL.

No, me !

THIRD.

Me rather !

FOURTH.

No, me !

FIRST GIRL
(*to Parsifal*).

Forbid'st thou me ?

SECOND.

Driv'st thou me back ?

FIRST.

Have women taught thee to fear them ?

SECOND.
Thyself wilt thou trust not near them ?

SEVERAL GIRLS.   .
What keeps thee thus so sluggish and chilly ?

OTHER GIRLS.
Are butterflies wooed by the rose or the lily ?

FIRST HALF.
He will not awaken !

A GIRL.
I leave him forsaken !

OTHERS.
By us to be taken !

OTHERS.
No, us ! — No, me ! —
Me too ! — Not thee ! —

PARSIFAL
(*half-angrily repulsing them and seeking to escape*).
Give o'er ! You catch me not !

(*From a thicket of flowers at the side is heard*)
KUNDRY'S VOICE.
Parsifal ! — Tarry !

(*The girls are frightened and at once become quiet. — Parsifal
stands as if spell-struck.*)

PARSIFAL.
Parsifal . . ?
So named me once in a dream my mother. —

Kundry's Voice.

Here linger, Parsifal ! —
With weal and bliss for thee comes my call. — —
You babe-hearted wooers, leave his side ;
    fast-withering flowers,
he was not for your pastime made !
    Go home, see to the wounded :
many a hero waits your aid.

The Girls

(slowly and reluctantly going from Parsifal).

Hence we scatter heavy-hearted,
    with grief, with grief we flee !
From all we freely could have parted,
    with him alone to be. —
        Farewell ! Farewell !
        Thou lurer ! Thou spurner !
        Thou — fool !

*(With the last words, amid soft laughter, they disappear
towards the castle.)*

Parsifal.

What happened — was it all a dream ?

*(He looks timidly round towards the side from whence the
voice came. There, by the parting of the foliage, has now become
visible a young woman of extreme beauty — Kundry, in
a completely altered form — lying upon a couch of flowers, and
lightly covered with fantastic clothing of a style approaching
the Arabian.)*

PARSIFAL

(*still at a distance*).

Me did'st thou call to, me the nameless?

KUNDRY.

I named thee, thee the fool-like Pure,
     " Fal parsi," —
    the spotless Fool-like, " Parsifal."
So called, when in Arabian land he died,
thy father Gamuret upon his son,
    whom, in his mother's womb yet hidden,
    with name of Parsifal he greeted.
To thee to tell it here in wait I stayed:
what brought thee, were it not the tidings' need?

PARSIFAL.

I never yet beheld or dreamed what now
I see, and what o'er-burdens me with dread. —
Hast thou too blossomed from the flower-thicket?

KUNDRY.

No, Parsifal, thou fool-like Pure!
    Wide — wide — from hence my home is : —
for thee to find me only am I here.
From farthest came I where I much beheld.
I saw the child upon his mother's breast,
his lisping still is laughter on my ear;
    though torn at heart,
    how laughed she too, at joy's behest,

when ceased her smart
and with the babe her eyes were blest ! —
On bedding mosses soft and deep,
whom she had fondled into sleep
and, wan with sorrow,
had watched all night in mother's-yearning,
he woke the morrow
with mother's-tears upon him burning.
She nothing was but woe and weeping
about thy father's love and death ;
to hold thee scathless in her keeping
was all for which she fed on breath :
from weapons far, from men of fight and madness,
hidden and safe to see thee was her gladness.
She nothing was but dread and prayer and trouble,
of news to fence from thee the lightest bubble.
Hear'st thou not still her wailing cry,
if late and far thou wert away ?
Hei ! How laughter flew to her mouth and her eye,
when lo she found thee in thy play !
When wild then around thee her arms were strained,
did'st thou shrink at her kisses as on thee they rained ?
Yet never reached thy ear her pain,
her frantic toil to find thee,
the day thou camest not again
and trace was none behind thee :
through nights and days she waited,
till words and wail abated,
in grief was drowned her smart,
for healing death she cried,
her sorrow broke her heart,
and — Herzeleide — died.

PARSIFAL

(with increasing emotion, till at last, terribly agitated, he sinks in grief at Kundry's feet).

Sorrow! Sorrow! What did I? Where was I?
Mother! Sweet, consoling mother!
Thy son, thy son was it who slew thee?
O fool! Blinded, staggering fool!
What led thee away lost and forgetful?
        Of thee, of thee forgetful,
        fondest, faithfullest mother?

KUNDRY

(still in recumbent position, bends over Parsifal's head, softly holds his brow and winds her arm fondly round his neck).

        Wert thou still free from smart,
                the bliss of healing
        could not befall thy heart:
        the rue, that makes it sore,
                shall fade from thy feeling
        'neath solace love can pour!

PARSIFAL
(troubled).

My mother, how had I heart to forget her?
Ha! Is there aught I forgot not as well?
What was I ever mindful of?
Of reckless foolhood I am full!

        (He lets himself sink lower and lower.)

KUNDRY.

        To once have told it,
        from sin its burden takes;
        to plain behold it,

of foolhood wisdom makes:
from love be not a flyer,
which folded Gamuret,
when Herzeleid' like fire
her arms about him set:
thy life and limb
love drew from him,
both death and foolhood quells its bliss;
through me
it brings to thee —
as latest mother's-blessing — this,
its first and freshest kiss.

(She has bent her head completely over his, and now fastens her lips, in a long kiss, upon his mouth.)

PARSIFAL

(leaps suddenly up with a gesture of extreme terror: his mien exhibits a fearful change; he presses his hands vehemently upon his heart, as if to stifle a lacerating pain; at last he breaks out).

Amfortas! — —
The wound! — The wound! —
Amid my heart it blazes. —
The woe-cry! The woe-cry!
The shattering woe-cry!
From deep within me leaps it aloft.
Oh! — Oh! —
Thou wretchedest! —
Thou woefullest! —
The wound, I saw it streaming: —
now bleeds it in myself —
here — here!

(While Kundry stares at him in terror and surprise, Parsifal, completely beyond himself, goes on:)

No, no! It is not the wound:
shed be its blood in fiery streams!
Here! Here, the blaze in my heart!
    The yearning, the merciless yearning,
that all my senses at once has seized!
    Oh! — Pang of love! —
How all upheaves and quails and quakes
    in surge of sinful longing! . . . .
            (*In shuddering whisper.*)
The hollow look is fixed upon the cup: —
    the holy blood within it glows; —
redemption-bliss as soft as heaven
abroad through every soul is shaken:
but here will wane not in my heart the wildness.
    Aloud I hear the Saver's sorrow —
        the groan to which it gathered —
    about the shrine so sore betrayed: —
        "redeem and loose me out
        from hands that sin has sullied!"
        So rang the groan of godhood
    loud and dreadly in my soul.
        And I? The fool, the coward?
To witless deeds of boyhood forth I fled!
        (*He sinks in despair upon his knees.*)
    Redeemer! Saver! Healing name!
    Amends how make I for the blame?

KUNDRY

(*whose wonder passes into passionate admiration, seeks timidly
to approach Parsifal*).

    From-high-sent hero! Away thy dream!
Look up and let thy Healer welcome seem!

PARSIFAL

(remaining in a bent position and looking vacantly up to Kundry while she stoops down to him and goes through the caressing movements which he here describes).

Yes! so it sounded when him she called; —
and such the look, plainly to me the same, —
and this the smile that so goadingly held him.
The lip . . . ah ! yes . . . so dimpled it at him ; —
so bent to him the bosom, —
so heaved itself the head ; —
so floated the hair in flashes ;
so ringed was his neck with the arm —
so swept him the cheek with its softness — !
In league with every pang of burning dole,
from heavenly weal
she kissed away his soul ! —
Ha ! — with this kiss !

(He has gradually raised himself, springs now fully up, and thrusts Kundry vehemently away.)

Undoer ! From me begone !
For ever — for ever — away !

KUNDRY

(in extreme passion).

Torturer ! — Ha ! —
Feel'st thou alone,
forgetting thy own,
of others the smart,
in thy god-filled heart
mine too let me teach thee to feel !

Art thou a Saver,
    what makes thee waver
  with me to be one for my weal?
From ere all time — for thee I wait, —
    the Saver, ah! so late,
    on whose thorn-goaded head
    I scorn once dared to shed. —
    Oh! Knew'st thou but the curse, —
    with sleep and with waking after,
      with death and life,
      and pain and laughter —
which, still to suffer strong and new,
the gulphs of being goads me through! —
    I looked on — Him — Him —
      with — laughter . . .
      then smote me his gaze. —
Now seek I him from world to world,
    till once again I meet him:
      when worst my need —
    already he seems to be near,
    his eyelight on me I feel: —
then back upon me comes the cursèd laughter, —
    a sinner sinks upon my bosom!
      Then laugh I — laugh I, —
      weep I cannot:
      I can but shriek,
      and rave and riot
in still fresh-falling madness-night
whence scarce I had woke by penance-might. —
Whom, faint for death, I yearned to light on,
whom straight I knew by saving power,
whom fell such blind and mocking slight on,

tears on his bosom let me shower.
with thee be one for a single hour,
and, ev'n by God and world off-cast,
in thee from sin be saved at last!

PARSIFAL.

For evermore
would'st thou with me be lost,
could I forget
the work that I was sent for,
an hour upon thy bosom! —
With weal for thee too I am here,
from love-sting if thou keepest clear.
The salves, whose touch will end thy pain,
yields not the well from which it flows:
thy search for weal is waste and vain
until that well to thee shall close;
another is it, — another, ah!
for which I wildly saw them yearn,
the brothers there, in pangs of dread
who make their bodies sore and dead.
But straight and plainly who can tell
the only weal's unfailing well?
Oh, sorrow! Flight of every stay!
How world and dream benight us!
Tow'rd highest weal the while we strongly pray, —
that thirst for hell's own fount should smite us!

KUNDRY.

My kiss if it was
that the world to thy sight has unclouded,
when locks thee my love's full-folding,
a god will my arms be holding!

The world redeem if such thou must :—
to godhood if here thou grow,
for that let me from heaven be thrust,
and endless be my woe !

PARSIFAL.

Redemption, sinner, I bring to thee too.

KUNDRY.

Thee let me love in thy godhood,
redemption thou bringest me then.

PARSIFAL.

Love and redemption both thou winnest, —
show'st thou me
to Amfortas hence the way.

KUNDRY

(breaking into rage).

Never — think thou to find him !
Who is fallen, leave him unfriended, —
the woe-sufferer,
shame-welcomer,
whom once I laughed at — laughed at — laughed at !
Ha ha ! When pricked him his proper spear !

PARSIFAL.

With holy lance to wound him who lacked the fear :

KUNDRY.

He, — He, —
who smote once low

the pride of my mocking spite, —
his curse — ha! — it gives me might;
on the spear I call to be also thy bane,
who hallow'st the sinner with fellow-pain! —
        Ha!   Madness! —
Suffer with me!   With me!
A single hour be mine, —
one hour let me be thine — :
        and forth to guide thee
shalt thou be shown a sign!

(She seeks to embrace him.   He thrusts her violently away.)

PARSIFAL.

Unblessèd woman, begone!

KUNDRY

(beats upon her breast and cries wildly towards the back).

Hither! Hither!   With help!
Hands to withhold him!   To me!
        Yield him no flight-way!
        Yield him no passage! —
And fled'st thou from here and foundest
all the ways of the world,
        the way that thou seek'st
should still be far from thee hidden!
        For path and passage,
        that hence may lead thee,
so — I curse them to thee:
        Stray-foot!   Stray-foot, —
        so well to me known —
I give thee to him for a guide!

(Klingsor has come out upon the wall: the girls also crowd out of the castle and seek to rush towards Kundry.)

KLINGSOR

(brandishing a spear).

Hold!   With the fitting tool I stay thee here:
the fool I catch upon his master's spear!

(He hurls the spear at Parsifal, over whose head it remains floating in the air; Parsifal seizes it in his hand and brandishes it with a gesture of intense exaltation indicating the form of the cross.)

PARSIFAL.

Behold the sign with which thy spell I wilder.
As the spear shall close
the wound that with it thou madest, —
in darkness and ruin
tumble thy treacherous show!

(The castle sinks as if by earthquake; the garden withers into a wilderness: the girls lie like faded flowers strewn upon the ground. — Kundry with a shriek has fallen to the earth.   To her once more, from the top of a fragment of the wall, the departing Parsifal turns.)

PARSIFAL.

Thou know'st —
where only thou wilt see me more!

(He disappears.   The curtain closes quickly.)

THIRD ACT.

In the realm of the Grail. — Open pleasant spring-landscape with flowery meadows rising softly towards the background. The foreground is occupied by the border of a wood extending towards the right. In the foreground at the wood-side a spring; opposite it, a little further down, a rough hermit-hut supported by a rock. Earliest morning. — Gurnemanz, as hermit, greatly aged, and meanly clad in the under-garment only of the grail-hood, enters from the hut and listens.

GURNEMANZ.

From yonder came the groaning. —
So woefully cries no beast,
and least of all this holiest morning here. —
I sure have heard this wailing sound before ?

(A hollow moaning, as of one in deep sleep troubled by dreams, is heard. — Gurnemanz walks straight to a densely overgrown thorn-thicket at the side; he forces it asunder: then stops suddenly.)

Ha ! She — here again ?
The thicket of wintry thorn
held her from sight : already how long ? —
Up ! — Kundry ! — Up !
The winter has fled and spring is here !
Awake, awake to the spring ! —
Cold — and stiff ! —

Dead, this time, I should deem her to be : —
but hers must have been the groaning I heard ?

*(He drags Kundry, quite stiff and lifeless, out of the bushes,
carries her to a neighbouring mound of turf, rubs her hands and
temples, breathes on her, and does all he can to dissipate her
numbness. At last she awakes. She is, precisely as in the
First Act, in the wild garb of the Grail-messenger : her complexion is, however, paler, and the wildness has vanished from
her features and demeanour. — She gazes long at Gurnemanz.
She then raises herself, puts her clothing and hair in order, and
prepares at once, like a maid, to set about her work.)*

GURNEMANZ.

Thou witless woman !
Hast thou no word for me ?
Is this thy thanks,
that I here awake thee
once more from thy deadly sleep ?

KUNDRY

(slowly lowers her head : then speaks in rough and broken tones).

Service . . service ! —

GURNEMANZ

(shakes his head).

Little of such is left !
On messages we send no more :
for herbs and roots
forage we each for himself ;
we learn of the beasts in the wood.

*(Kundry has meanwhile looked around, notices the hut and
goes in.)*

GURNEMANZ

(looking after her with surprise).

How otherwise she walks than of old !
Works on her so the holy day ?
Oh ! Day of grace to all free-given !
 For weal to her it happens
 that out of her to-day
 the death-sleep I have driven.

(Kundry comes again out of the hut ; she carries a pitcher and goes with it to the spring. While she awaits its filling she looks into the wood and sees in the distance some one coming ; she turns to Gurnemanz to call his attention to the fact.)

GURNEMANZ

(looking into the wood).

Who yonder walks to the holy well ?
 In gloomy weapon-harness,
 none of the brothers is it.

(Kundry moves slowly off with the filled pitcher to the hut, and busies herself inside. — Gurnemanz in wonder goes a little aside to watch the new-comer. — Parsifal enters from the wood. He is entirely in black armour ; with closed helmet and lowered spear, his head bent, he walks slowly and dreamily along, and seats himself on the little mound of turf by the spring.)

GURNEMANZ

(watches him for some time, and then goes a little nearer).

 Hail to thee here, my guest !
Lost is thy way, and shall I befriend thee ?

(Parsifal gently shakes his head.)

GURNEMANZ.

No greeting to me wilt thou give ?

(*Parsifal bows his head.*)

GURNEMANZ.

Hei ! — What ? —
If the vow, that binds thee,
has brought thee to this thy dumbness,
the oath I am under bids me
to tell thee plainly what befits. —
Here art thou on a holy spot :
no passer comes with weapons here,
with bolted helmet, shield and spear.
This morning too !   Know'st thou then not
what holy day it is ?

(*Parsifal shakes his head.*)

So !   From whence com'st thou then ?
What heathen hast thou dwelt amid,
who know'st not that to-day
all-blest-and-holy-held Good-Friday is ?

(*Parsifal sinks his head still lower.*)

Put off thy weapons !
Vex not the Lord who, lone and naked,
the treasure of his holy blood
shed for the sinful world to-day !

(*Parsifal rises after a further silence, sticks the spear into the
ground before him, lays shield and sword at its foot, opens his
helmet, takes it from his head and puts it with the other arms,
then kneels before the spear in silent prayer.   Gurnemanz
watches him with astonishment and emotion.   He beckons to
Kundry, who has just come out of the hut. — Parsifal
earnestly praying now raises his eyes with devotion towards
the point of the spear.*)

GURNEMANZ

(softly to Kundry).

Beholdest thou ? . .
'Tis he who slaughtered once the swan.

(Kundry nods her head gently.)

None else than he !
The fool, that in wrath I thrust away !
Ha! To what halt-place came he ?
The spear, — I know it well.

(With great emotion.)

Oh ! — Holiest day,
to which I here have lived to wake !

(Kundry has turned away her face.)

PARSIFAL

(rises slowly from his prayer, looks calmly round, recognizes Gurnemanz, and stretches his hand gently to him).

Blest am I to again have found thee !

GURNEMANZ.

Still see'st thou who I am ?
Of me art mindful,
whom grief and need so deep have bowed ?
How cam'st thou to-day ?   From whence ?

PARSIFAL.

By ways of search and suffering I came ;
if even yet I dare to deem them ended,
when here again the forest
greets me with its rustle,

and thou, good father, giv'st me welcome ?
    Or . . . am I still but wand'ring ?
    All looks to have been altered.

GURNEMANZ.

But say to whom the way thou soughtest ?

PARSIFAL.

    To him, whose heart-poured woe-cry
I, fool-like, once with wonder heard ;
    to whom this day with healing
I dare believe myself am sent.
        But — ah ! —
far from the path of weal to keep me,
        through passageless tangles
drove me a wildering curse astray :
        toils without number,
        battles and struggles
    back from the way still forced me,
    soon as I fancied it found.
    Then fierce unhopefulness seized me
    that safe my charge I should harbour,
whose holiness from foes to shelter
I wounds from every weapon have borne.
        For not itself
    I dared in battle to wield it :
        free from fleck
    I sought at my side to shield it,
    till home to-day I yield it :
behold it safe and shining here, —
    the Grailhood's holy spear !

Gurnemanz.

Oh, welfare! Topmost grace!
Oh, wonder! Holy highest wonder!
   (*After he has a little composed himself.*)
   But, Lord! was it a curse
that drove thee from the rightful way,
   believe me, it is over.
Here art thou; here where sways the Grail,
and for thee all its Knighthood waits.
   Ah! there is need of healing,
   the healing that thou bring'st! —
For since the day that here thou madest halt,
   the sorrow that thou then beheldest,
   the sickness — to its height has wrought:
Amfortas, with his wound o'er-maddened,
to still the pangs his soul was sore with,
for death, in frantic stubbornness, besought:
   no prayers, no woes amid the Knighthood,
could move him more to lead the holy service.
Within its shrine has long been shut the Grail:
   thus hopes its sin-bewailing keeper,
      since still he cannot die
      while it he ever sees,
      his end by force to hasten,
and with his life his pain at once to finish.
The holy meal for us is never set,
   on common food we have to fare,
which brings our heroes into heartless plight:
   of news we get no sound,
or call from far to deeds of holy battle:
   wan and wretched lags around
the Knighthood without leadership or might.

Here in the wood I hide myself alone,
    for death each day more ready,
to whom my hoary weapon-lord has fallen ;
    for Titurel, my holy hero,
when sight no longer of the Grail he fed on,
    he died, — a man like others !

PARSIFAL
(*with a start of sudden grief*).
    And I — 't is I,
who all this woe have wrought !
    Ha ! of what mischief,
    what sin, the blame
must here on this fool-head
have weighed from everlasting,
since never sorrow, never penance
from bane of blindness could restore me !
Whom Heav'n to work of ransom chose,
in maze and madness seems to close
the last-left ransom-path before me !

(*He seems about to fall insensible. Gurnemanz supports him,
and helps him to seat himself on the mound of turf. — Kundry
has fetched a basin with water to sprinkle Parsifal.*)

GURNEMANZ
(*putting Kundry aside*).
    Not so ! —
    The holy well itself
shall fresher make our pilgrim's bath.
    I lofty work forebode
    that yet to-day awaits him
as leader of a holy service :
    so cleansed be he from stain,

and lengthened wandering's dust
shall now from him be washed again.

(Parsifal is by both of them turned gently towards the border
of the spring. While Kundry loosens his greaves and then
bathes his feet, Gurnemanz takes off his corslet for him.)

PARSIFAL

(faintly and low).

Amfortas shall I yet to-day be led to?

GURNEMANZ

(while they are tending him).

The Grail-burg yonder waits us even now :
the grave-rites of my old belovèd lord
          sore-hearted call me thither.
The Grail once further for us to unmuffle,
     in the long-unwonted service
     once more to-day to lead us —
that hallowed may be made his father,
who sank beneath the guilt which now
his grieving son would thus atone,—
     Amfortas gave his word.

PARSIFAL.

(regarding Kundry with wonder).

My feet since thou hast watered, —
the friend here . . . let him dew my head.

GURNEMANZ

(taking water in his hand from the spring and sprinkling
Parsifal's head).

Be hallowed, thou unspotted, by the spotless !
          Of every blame begone
          the burden from thee now !

(During the action of Gurnemanz Kundry has drawn a golden phial from her bosom and poured part of its contents over Parsifal's feet; she now quickly loosens her hair and wipes them with it.)

PARSIFAL

(takes the phial from her).

The feet she washed, behold, she now has ointed;
my head the mate of Titurel shall balm,
that yet to-day as King he here may hail me.

GURNEMANZ

(pours the whole remaining contents of the phial upon Parsifal's head, which he rubs softly, and then folds his hands over it).

So promised was it we should treat thee;
　　　　so hallow I thy head,
　　　　as King that I may greet thee.
　　　　　　Thou — Spotless!
Sufferer of fellow-pain,
learner of the healing deed!
Since thou hast felt his pangs whom thou redeemest,
the latest load now loosen from his head.

PARSIFAL

(unobserved takes water from the spring, bends over Kundry, who is still kneeling before him, and wets her head).

　　My foremost charge fulfil I so: —
　　　　be thou baptised,
　　　　believe in the Redeemer!

(Kundry sinks her head low towards the ground and seems to weep vehemently.)

Parsifal

(turns round and looks, rapt and tenderly, at forest and meadow).

How fair to-day the fields before me seem ! —
    With wonder-flowers once I met
that wound me to the head in clinging garlands ;
    yet never looked so soft and still
        the grass, the blossoms and flowers,
    nor sent me so childhoodlike a smell,
    nor spoke so heart-to-heart with me.

Gurnemanz.

That is Good-Friday's-wonder, Lord !

Parsifal.

Alas, the day of every grief !
The day, meseems, when all that blooms,
that breathes, and lives and lives again,
    should weep and show but sadness ?

Gurnemanz.

    Thou see'st it is not so. —
The sinner's tears of sorrow is it
    that sprinkle field and plain
    to-day with holy rain,
    in which they thus have thriven.
Each living thing upon its place
is glad at the Redeemer's trace,
    to whom in prayer its thanks are given ;
to see him on the cross is not its dower :
so looks it up to man whom he redeemed,
who feels himself unyoked from sin's and terror's power,
by God's love-offering unstained and whole :

5

now feel, upon the meadows, grass and flower
that foot of man to-day they need not dread;
but lo, as God in his long-suffering
  had thought of man and for him bled,
so man to-day has care for everything,
      and tender makes his tread.
  Thankful are things of every name
  that bloom and fleetly fade away,
  the world, unburdened of its blame, —
  of sinlessness has earned its day.

*(Kundry has slowly again raised her head, and with moistened
and prayerful eyes looks earnestly and calmly up to Parsifal.)*

PARSIFAL.

Who smiled on me, I saw them wither:
to-day for healing yearn they hither?—
Thy eyes, as well, a dew of blessing yield:
  thou weepest — lo! how laughs the field.

(He kisses her softly on the forehead.)

(A distant sound of bells, gradually swelling.)

GURNEMANZ.

  Mid-day. —
  The hour is here: —
be granted, Lord, that hence thy server lead thee! —

*(Gurnemanz has fetched a tabard and mantle of the Grailhood;
he and Kundry dress Parsifal in them. The scene changes very
gradually, in the same way as in the First Act, only from right
to left. Parsifal solemnly grasps the spear and with Kundry
slowly follows Gurnemanz who leads the way. — After the
wood has quite vanished, and doors in the rock have opened
through which the three have disappeared, trains of knights in*

*funeral-garments are seen in the vaulted passages and a con-
tinually increasing sound of bells is heard. — At last the great
hall, as in the First Act, only without the tables, re-appears.
It is dimly lighted. The doors again open. From one side
enter the knights carrying Titurel's body in a coffin. On the
other side Amfortas is brought in on his litter, with the veiled
casket of the " Grail" borne before him. In the midst the
catafalk, behind it the raised seat under the baldacchino, upon
which Amfortas is again placed.)*

(*Singing of the knights during their entry.*)

FIRST TRAIN OF KNIGHTS

(*with the " Grail" and Amfortas*).

While here we carry in covering shrine
 the Grail to holy service,
whom cover you in gloomy shrine
 and bring in sorrow along ?

SECOND TRAIN

(*with Titurel's coffin*).

The grave-shrine covers the hero here,
 it covers the holy might
to whose keeping God once gave himself:
 Titurel bear we along.

FIRST TRAIN.

What slew him, who, under the eye of God,
 God himself once guarded ?

SECOND TRAIN.

He fell by the burden of killing age
 when the Grail he beheld no longer.

FIRST TRAIN.

From sight of the Grail who was it then that barred him ?

SECOND TRAIN.

Whom yonder you carry, its sinful keeper.

FIRST TRAIN.

We bring him to-day, for to-day once further
— and never after! —
he girds himself to the service.

SECOND TRAIN.

Sorrow! Sorrow! Thou guard of our weal!
For the latest time
in mind of thy charge be put!

(*The coffin is laid upon the catafalk, and Amfortas upon the couch.*)

AMFORTAS.

Yea, sorrow! Sorrow! Sorrow to me! —
So wail I freely with you:
freelier death at your hands I would take,
for sin the easiest penance!

(*The coffin has been opened. At the sight of Titurel's corpse all break into a sharp cry of lamentation.*)

AMFORTAS

(*raising himself high up from the couch, and turning towards the corpse*).

My father!
High and blessèd among heroes,
whose holiness drew to thee once the angels!
While death I hungered to suffer,
thine was the life I took!

Oh! Thou, who now in heavenly light
    the Redeemer's self beholdest,
by prayer from him wring that his holy blood,
    when for-once-again its blessing
    it sheds upon the brothers,
    as life anew to their bodies,
    at last may yield to me — death!
        Death! — To die!
        Grace beyond measure!
Away let the wound and its venom be stifled,
the heart that it feeds on grow pulseless and cold!
    My father! Thee — I cry to,
    cry thou in turn to him:
" Redeemer, at length to my son give rest!"

THE KNIGHTS
(pressing in disorder closer to Amfortas).
    Unmuffle the shrine! —
    Quick to the service!
    So bids thee thy father: —
    thou must, thou must!

AMFORTAS
*(leaping up in rage and despair, and flinging himself among
the knights as they fall back).*
    No! — No more! — Ha! —
Already with death my soul is darkened, —
and again to life shall I tear myself back?
    What wilders you!
    Who is there should force me to live?
    'T is death that alone you can give!
      (He tears open his garment.)

Here am I, — the gaping wound is here!
The blood that eats me, behold it flow!
Your swords unshackle! Bury your weapons
deep — deep in it, over the hilt!
     You heroes, up!
Slaughter the sinner here in his woe:
of itself the Grail to you then will glow!

(All have fallen back from him. Amfortas stands, in a state of terrible exaltation, alone. — Parsifal, accompanied by Gurnemanz and Kundry, has unnoticed mixed himself among the knights; he now steps forward and extends the spear, with the point of which he touches the side of Amfortas.)

PARSIFAL.

One only weapon fits : —
     the spear alone,
that made it, shuts the wound.

(The features of Amfortas light up with holy ecstasy: he seems about to sink with the force of his emotion : Gurnemanz supports him.)

PARSIFAL.

Be whole, forgiven and unstained!
For now thy charge from thee I take. —
     Thy suffering be hallowed,
by which the highest strength of fellow-pain
     and sheerest wisdom's might
     were taught the backward fool.
          The holy spear
     I bring you home again. —

(All fix their eyes with highest rapture upon the uplifted spear, while Parsifal, raising his look to its point, continues as though inspired :)

Oh! Blessèd wonder, great and plain! —
The point, that on thy wound had power, . . .
unearthly blood behold it shower,
which yearns its kindred stream to follow
into the Grail's all-holy hollow! —
No more shall it forbear to shine:
unwrap the Grail! Open the shrine!

(*The boys open the casket: Parsifal takes from it the " Grail"
and, with silent prayer, buries himself in contemplation of it.
The " Grail" glows: a gleam of glory spreads itself over all. —
Titurel, for the moment brought again to life, rises, with a gesture
of blessing, in his coffin. — From the dome comes down a white
dove which remains floating over Parsifal's head. He swings
the " Grail" softly before the upraised looks of the Knighthood. —
Kundry, with her eyes lifted to him, sinks slowly lifeless before
Parsifal to the ground. Amfortas and Gurnemanz fall
reverently on their knees at Parsifal's feet.*)

ALL

(*accompanied by scarcely audible voices out of the mid and
topmost height*).

Highest healing's Wonder:
salvation to the Saver!

(*The curtain closes.*)

"THE NIBELUNG'S RING."

MR. ALFRED FORMAN'S VERSION OF "DER RING DES NIBELUNGEN."

The only one approved by Wagner, and the first translation into any language.

~~~~~~~~~~~~~~~~~~~~~~~~~~~~~~

Richard Wagner :—

. . . . Für diesen Eifer und diese Liebe sage ich Ihnen meinen wärmsten Dank, und soll es mich sehr freuen wenn Sie diese schöne Arbeit dem Wagner-Verein und ins besondere meinem Freund Herrn Dannreuther übergeben.

Algernon Charles Swinburne :—

I do not wonder at the cordiality of commendation bestowed by the Master on such a version of his great work.

Theodore Watts-Dunton :—

An admirable translation. Mr. Forman's task was enormously difficult, and his success can scarcely be exaggerated.

Richard Garnett :—

Mr. Forman's translation is a marvellous *tour de force*. I have been reading it with very great pleasure.

Hans von Bülow :—

A most marvellous translation.

John Payne :—

Mr. Alfred Forman has successfully accomplished a task which might rebut the boldest of translators.

Edward Dannreuther :—

Forman's translation was a labour of love. He never departs from the form or spirit of the original.

Athenæum :—

Intending visitors to the performances of Wagner's colossal work cannot be too strongly urged to peruse Mr. Alfred Forman's admirable translation of the poem.

Academy :—

The extraordinary difficulty of the task may be imagined when it is said that not merely is the English version fitted to the music, the rhythm and metre being closely adhered to, but that even the alliterative verse has been preserved in the translation.

Standard :—

The spirit of the poem can best be seized through Mr. Forman's really admirable translation.

Daily News :—

A very close translation.

Morning Post :—

Mr. Forman has been deservedly praised by Wagner and Von Bülow for the excellence of his work.

Daily Chronicle :—

In Mr. Forman's work we are borne into an ideal sphere. We wonder at the wealth of pregnant words; we are entranced by the unity of style and feeling; and under his guidance we traverse the new world of poetry which Wagner himself has revealed to us.

Globe :—

Mr. Forman's version supplies a public want. It has the merit of following the original very closely, both in meaning and form.

St. James's Gazette :—

Mr. Forman has produced what must in itself be regarded as a fine poem.

Evening News :—

Mr. Alfred Forman's admirable translation of the gigantic tetralogy, "Der Ring des Nibelungen," is entitled to rank as a valuable contribution to the dramatic literature of the day.

Court Circular :—

Wagner is to be greatly congratulated on having found an interpreter who has recognised in "Der Ring des Nibelungen" a tragic poem of the first importance, and who has rendered it into English in such a manner as to convey the same impression.

Weekly Dispatch :—

A splendid translation. . . . Mr. Forman's task has evidently been a labour of love.

Weekly Times :—

The diction of Mr. Forman's translation is everywhere marked by that inventive and organising sense of language which is the gift of only a born poet.

London Figaro :—

An admirable English adaptation. . . . This was the version approved by Wagner.

Society :—

In Mr. Alfred Forman's translation, the alliterative beauty and Teutonic strength of the original have been preserved in a manner that is simply marvellous.

Musical Standard :—

The philological import of Mr. Forman's work is as great as its poetic charm. We rise from perusal of the transcription with the consciousness that we have passed through the same world and received the same impressions as during our reading of the original.

Musical World :—

A masterly version, or rather marvellous counterpart of the original.

Musical Times :—

None but a genuine enthusiast would have dreamed of undertaking so herculean a work as this translation. . . . It can be honestly recommended as giving an excellent idea both of the spirit and form of the work.

Manchester Examiner :—

Mr. Alfred Forman's version is at once a poem in itself, and one in which the spirit of the original is faithfully reproduced.

Northern Echo :—

To have failed in such an undertaking would have been to have excited admiration for the boldness of the attempt. To have succeeded is a felicity any Englishman of letters might envy.

The Meister :—

A work too fine to need our praise.

Vienna Neues Fremden-Blatt :—

The existence of so valuable a translation as Forman's should serve to spread continually wider and wider the interest in and the understanding of Wagner's creations in England.

Glasenapp's "Life of Wagner" :—

The translation of the poem of "Der Ring des Nibelungen," by Alfred Forman, has the reputation of being a work of monumental importance.

"TRISTAN AND ISOLDE."

MR. ALFRED FORMAN'S TRANSLATION OF "TRISTAN UND ISOLDE."

Theodore Watts-Dunton :—

An admirable translation.

W. Ashton Ellis, in the "Musical World" :—

We feel justified in ranking this translation even higher than Mr. Forman's own version of the *Ring*. . . . The manner in which the rhyme, the alliteration, and the rhythm of the original have been preserved, is beyond all praise. The music seems to have leapt from the score into the text. . . . We may fairly say that, had Richard Wagner been an Englishman, these are the words that he would have chosen wherewith to clothe his thoughts.

Charles Dowdeswell, in the "Artist" :—

Mr. Forman has first of all securely captured the secret of the poem, its deeply hidden nature, its spiritual essence. The other English translators have worked away at the dress in which the poem is clothed without having made anything but a superficial acquaintance with the living body behind it. . . . Mr. Forman has thoroughly possessed himself of the work's metaphysical heart, its profoundly beautiful philosophy, its world - embracing import. Combined with this uncommon faculty of insight are to be found an ample technical equipment, viz., the flexible use of a rich poetic vocabulary, a power of idiomatic reproduction, and a well-controlled but invariably present energy.

Musical World :—

The work has the air of an original poem of great strength and individuality. The feelings aroused by its perusal are similar, not only in nature but in strength, to those evoked by a reading of the original poem.

The Meister :—

A most faithful representative of the original, and it is marked by that happy facility for rendering into English the sound, the accent and the flavour of the original, which Mr. Forman so pre-eminently possesses.

Modern Art and Literature :—

All other English adaptations of Wagner's music-dramas, or tone-poems, seem bald and commonplace when compared with Mr. Forman's translations. The dexterity with which he has fitted German idioms with English equivalents, preserving, by some magic of his own, the most subtle shades of meaning, has gained the admiration of linguists and philologists of all degrees.